To Eileen and Maria

Atheneum Books for Young Readers
An imprint of Simon & Schuster Children's Publishing Division
1230 Avenue of the Americas, New York, NY 10020

Copyright © 1994 by Gerald Fitzgerald

The text of this book is set in Kennerly.
The illustrations are rendered in acrylic.

First U.S. edition, 1995

Originally published in Great Britain by ABC, All Books for Children

Printed in Singapore

10 9 8 7 6 5 4 3 2 1

Library of Congress Catalog Card Number: 94-71917

ISBN 0-689-31945-2

Casey at the Bat

by Ernest Lawrence Thayer
illustrated by Gerald Fitzgerald

Atheneum Books for Young Readers

The outlook wasn't brilliant for the
   Mudville nine that day;
The score stood four to two with but
   one inning more to play;
And then, when Cooney died at first,
   and Barrows did the same,
A sickly silence fell upon the patrons
   of the game.

A straggling few got up to go,
in deep despair. The rest
Clung to that hope which
    "springs eternal in the human breast";
They thought, If only Casey
    could but get a whack at that,
We'd put up even money now,
    with Casey at the bat.

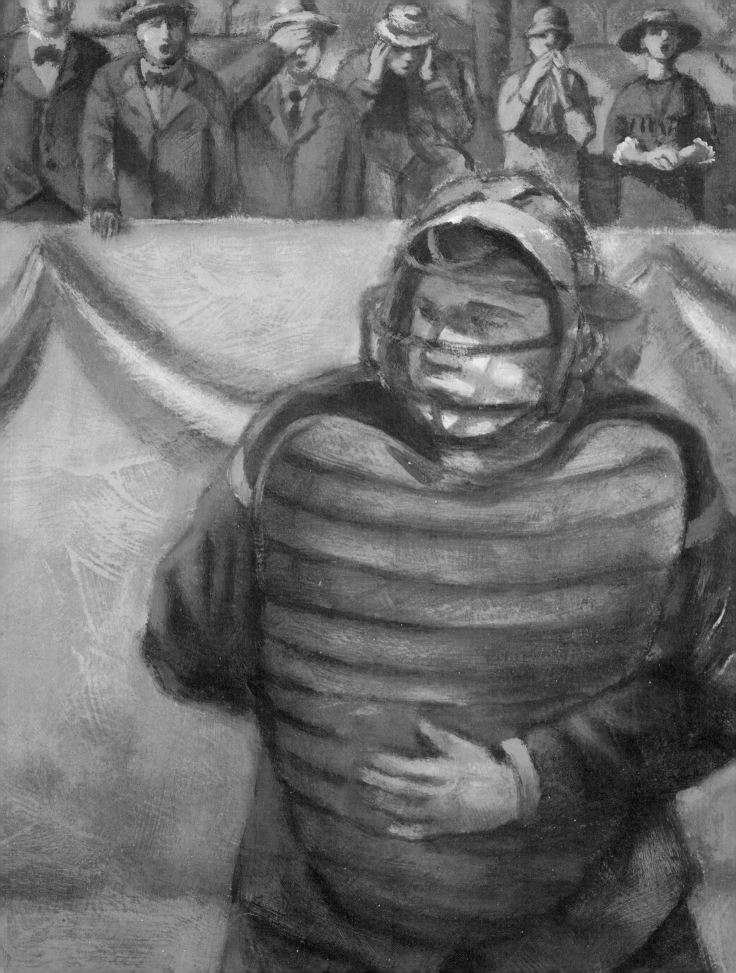

But Flynn preceded Casey, as did
    also Jimmy Blake,
And the former was a lulu and the
    latter was a cake;

So, upon that stricken multitude grim
    melancholy sat,
For there seemed but little chance of
    Casey's getting to the bat.

But Flynn let drive a single, to the
wonderment of all,
And Blake, the much despised, tore
the cover off the ball,

And when the dust had lifted and
men saw what had occurred,
There was Jimmy safe at second,
and Flynn a-huggin' third.

Then from five thousand
throats and more
there rose a lusty yell,
It rumbled through the valley;
it rattled in the dell;
It knocked upon the mountain
and recoiled upon the flat,
For Casey, mighty Casey,
was advancing to the bat.

There was ease in Casey's manner
as he stepped into his place;
There was pride in Casey's bearing
and a smile on Casey's face,
And when, responding to the cheers,
he lightly doffed his hat,
No stranger in the crowd could doubt
'twas Casey at the bat.

Ten thousand eyes were on him as he
    rubbed his hands with dirt;
Five thousand tongues applauded when
    he wiped them on his shirt.

Then, while the writhing pitcher ground
    the ball into his hip,
Defiance gleamed in Casey's eye, a sneer
    curled Casey's lip.
And now the leather-covered sphere came
    hurtling through the air,
And Casey stood a-watching it in haughty
    grandeur there.
Close by the sturdy batsman the ball
    unheeded sped –
"That ain't my style," said Casey.
"Strike one," the umpire said.

From the benches, black with people,
 there went up a muffled roar,
Like the beating of the storm-waves
 on a stern and distant shore.
"Kill him; kill the umpire!" shouted
 someone from the stand –
And it's likely they'd have killed him
 had not Casey raised his hand.

With a smile of Christian charity
    great Casey's visage shone;
He stilled the rising tumult; he
    bade the game go on;
He signaled to the pitcher, and
    once more the spheroid flew;
But Casey still ignored it, and
    the umpire said, "Strike two."

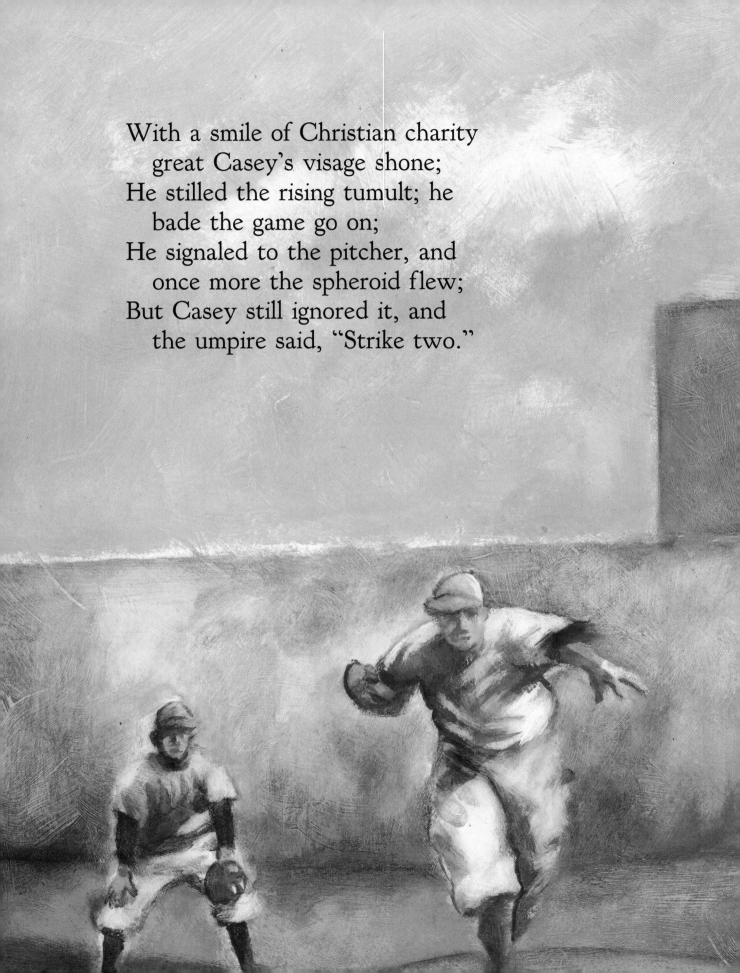

"Fraud," cried the maddened thousands,
   and echo answered "Fraud,"
But one scornful look from Casey,
   and the multitude was awed.
They saw his face grow stern and cold;
   they saw his muscles strain,
And they knew that Casey wouldn't
   let that ball go by again.

The sneer is gone from Casey's lip;
his teeth are clinched in hate;
He pounds with cruel violence
his bat upon the plate.
And now the pitcher holds the ball,
and now he lets it go,
And now the air is shattered
by the force of Casey's blow.

Oh! somewhere in this favored land
the sun is shining bright;
The band is playing somewhere,
and somewhere hearts are light.
And somewhere men are laughing,
and somewhere children shout;
But there is no joy in Mudville –
mighty Casey has Struck Out.

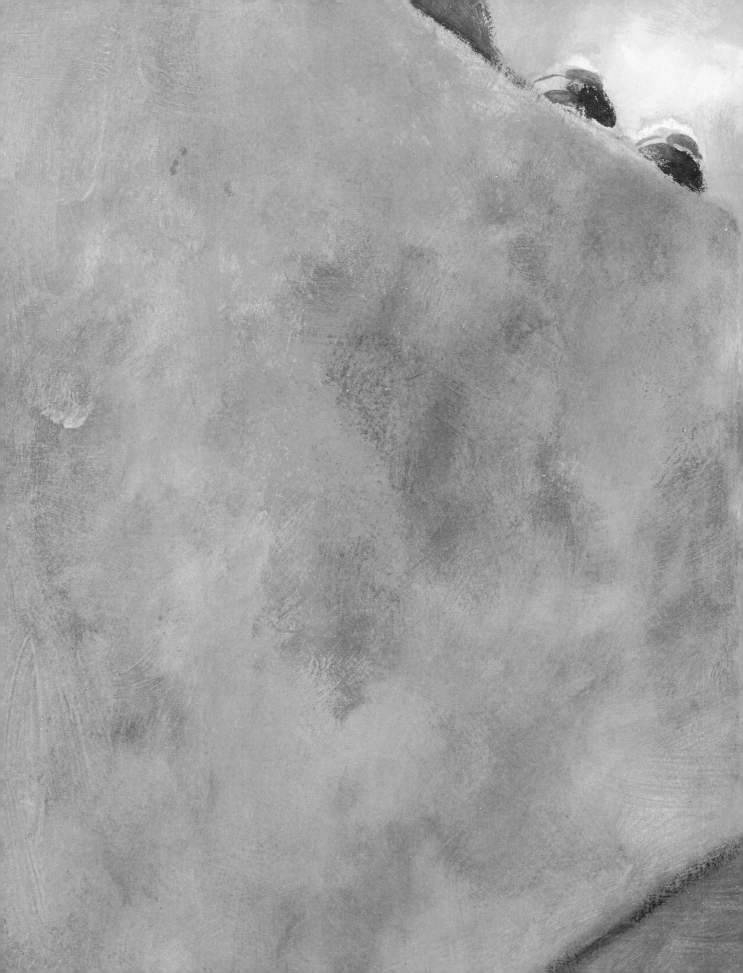